The Clean House

by Sarah Ruhl

A SAMUEL FRENCH ACTING EDITION

SAMUEL FRENCH

FOUNDED 1830

New York Hollywood London Toronto

SAMUELFRENCH.COM

ISBN   978-0-573-63398-0   Printed   in   U.S.A.   #6266

IMPORTANT BILLING AND CREDIT
REQUIREMENTS

All producers of *THE CLEAN HOUSE* must give credit to the Author of the Play and the Author of the Novel in all programs distributed in connection with performances of the Play and in all instances in which the title of the Play appears for purposes of advertising, publicizing or otherwise exploiting the Play and/or a production. The name of the Author of the Play *must* appear on a separate line on which no other name appears, immediately following the title, and must appear in size of type not less than fifty percent the size of the title type. The name of the Author of the Novel must appear on a separate line immediately below the Name of the Author of the Play in a size of type equal to that of the Author of the Play, wherever and whenever the Author of the Play receives credit.

In addition the following special billing must appear also appear:

"World Priemiere of THE CLEAN HOUSE was produced by
Yale Repertory Theatre, New Haven, Connecticut
James Bundy, artistic Director; Victoria Nolan, Managing Director"

"Produced by Lincoln Center Theater in 2006
New York City"

And on a separate line and less prominently shall read the following additional credit:

First Act Commissioned by McCarter Theatre

THE CLEAN HOUSE had its World Premiere at the Yale Repertory Theatre, New Haven, Connecticut, James Bundy, artistic Director; Victoria Nolan, Managing Director, on September 23rd, 2004. The creative team included scenic designer Christopher Acebo, costume designer Shigeru Yaji, lighting designer Geoff Korf, sound designer and composer Andre Pluess, vocal coach Stephen Gabis, dramaturg Rachel Rusch, and production stage manager James Mountcastle. The prodcution was directed by Bill Rauch with the following cast:

MATILDE......................................Zilah Mendoza
LANE......................................Elizabeth Norment
VIRGINIA..................................Laurie Kennedy
A MAN/CHARLES.............................Tom Bloom
A WOMAN/ANA.......Carmen De Lavallade/Franca Barchiesi

THE CLEAN HOUSE subsequently opened at the at the Mitzi E. Newhouse Theater at the Lincoln Center Theatre, André Bishop, Artistic Director, Bernard Gersten, Executive Producer on October 5th , 2006. Set design was by Christopher Acebo, with Costumes by Shigeru Yaji, and Lighting by James F. Ingalls. The Sound Designer/Composer was André Pluess and the Choreographer was Sabrina Peck. The production was directed by Bill Rauch with the following cast:

MATILDE................................Vanessa Aspillaga
LANE..Blair Brown
VIRGINIA..................................Jill Clayburgh
A MAN/CHARLES..........................John Dossett
A WOMAN/ANA...........................Concetta Tomei

THE CLEAN HOUSE
was a Pulitzer Prize Finalist
and
won the 2004 Susan Smith Blackburn Prize

CHARACTERS

LANE, a doctor, a woman in her early fifties. She wears white.

MATILDE, Lane's cleaning lady, a woman in her late twenties. She wears black. She is Brazilian. She has a refined sense of deadpan.

VIRGINIA, Lane's sister, a woman in her late fifties.

CHARLES, Lane's husband, a man in his fifties. A compassionate surgeon. He is childlike underneath his white coat. In the first act, Charles plays Matilde's father.

ANA, a woman who is older than Lane. She is Argentinean. She is impossibly charismatic. In the first act she plays Matilde's mother.

*NOTE: Everyone in this play should
be able to tell a really good joke.*

PLACE

A white living room.
White couch, white vase, white lamp, white rug.

A balcony.

PLACE

A metaphysical Connecticut. Or, a house that is not far from the city and not far from the sea.

This play is dedicated to the doctors in my life,
Tony and Kate.

ACT ONE

1. Matilde

Matilde tells a long joke in Portuguese to the audience.*
We can tell she is telling a joke even though we might not understand
the language.
She finishes the joke.
She exits.

2. Lane

Lane, to the audience.

LANE. It has been such a hard month.

My cleaning lady—from Brazil—decided that she was depressed one day and stopped cleaning my house.

I was like:

clean my house!

And she wouldn't!

We took her to the hospital and I had her medicated and she

---

*See page 89 of the Production Notes

7

Still Wouldn't Clean.

And—in the meantime—*I've* been cleaning my house!

I'm sorry, but I did not go to medical school to clean my own house.

3. Virginia

Virginia, to the audience.

VIRGINIA. People who give up the *privilege* of cleaning their own houses—they're insane people.

If you do not clean: how do you know if you've made any progress in life? I love dust. The dust always makes progress. Then I remove the dust. That is progress.

If it were not for dust I think I would die. If there were no dust to clean then there would be so much leisure time and so much thinking time and I would have to do something besides thinking and that thing might be to slit my wrists.

Ha ha ha ha ha ha just kidding.

I'm not a morbid person. That just popped out!

My sister is a wonderful person. She's a doctor. At an important hospital. I've always wondered how one hospital can be more important than another hospital. They are places for human waste. Places to put dead bodies.

I'm sorry. I'm being morbid again.

My sister has given up the privilege of cleaning her own house. Something deeply personal—she has given up. She does not know *cold*

how long it takes the dust to accumulate under her bed. She does not know if her husband is sleeping with a prostitute because she does not smell his dirty underwear. All of these things, she fails to know.

I know when there is dust on the mirror. Don't misunderstand me—I'm an educated woman. But if I were to die at any moment during the day, no one would have to clean my kitchen.

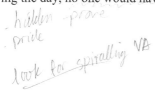

- hidden -prove
- pride
look for spiralling VA

4. Matilde

Matilde, to the audience.

MATILDE. The story of my parents is this. It was said that my father was the funniest man in his village. He did not marry until he was sixty-three because he did not want to marry a woman who was not funny. He said he would wait until he met his match in wit.

And then one day he met my mother. He used to say: your mother—and he would take a long pause— *(Matilde takes a long pause)*—is funnier than I am. We have never been apart since the day we met, because I always wanted to know the next joke.

My mother and father did not look into each other's eyes. They laughed like hyenas. Even when they made love they laughed like hyenas. My mother was old for a mother. She refused many proposals. It would kill her, she said, to have to spend her days laughing at jokes that were not funny.

Pause.

I wear black because I am in mourning. My mother died last year. Have you ever heard the expression 'I almost died laughing?' Well that's what she did. The doctors couldn't explain it. They argued, they said she choked on her own spit, but they don't really know. She was laughing at one of my father's jokes. A joke he took one year to make up, for the anniversary of their marriage. When my mother died laughing, my father shot himself. And so I came here, to clean this house.

5. Lane and Matilde

Lane enters.
Matilde is looking out the window.

> LANE. Are you all right?
> MATILDE. Yes.
> LANE. Would you please clean the bathroom when you get a chance?
> MATILDE. Yes.
> LANE. Soon?
> MATILDE. Yes.

Matilde looks at Lane.

> LANE. The house is very dirty.

Matilde is silent.

LANE. This is difficult for me. I don't like to order people around. I've never had a live-in maid.

Matilde is silent.

LANE. Matilde—what did you do in your country before you came to the United States?

MATILDE. I was a student. I studied humor. You know—jokes.

LANE. I'm being serious.

MATILDE. I'm being serious too. My parents were the funniest people in Brazil. And then they died.

LANE. I'm sorry. That must be very difficult.

MATILDE. I was the third funniest person in my family. Then my parents died, making me the first funniest. It is terrible to be the first funniest, so I left.

LANE. That's very interesting. I don't—always—understand the arts. Listen. Matilde. I understand that you have a life, an emotional life—and that you are also my cleaning lady. If I met you at—say—a party—and you said, I am from a small village in Brazil, and my parents were comedians, I would say: that's very interesting. You sound like a very interesting woman.

But life is about context.

And I have met you in the context of my house, where I have hired you to clean. And I don't want an interesting person to clean my house. I just want my house—cleaned.

Lane is on the verge of tears.

MATILDE. Is something wrong?

LANE. No, it's just that—I don't like giving orders in my own *professional life + home life uncomfortable* (handwritten annotation)

home. It makes me—uncomfortable. I want you to do all the things I want you to do without my having to tell you.

MATILDE. Do you tell the nurses at the hospital what to do?

LANE. Yes.

MATILDE. Then pretend I am your nurse.

LANE. Okay.

Nurse—would you polish the silver, please.

MATILDE. A doctor does not say: Nurse—would you polish the silver, please. A doctor says: Nurse—polish the silver.

LANE. You're right. Nurse: polish the silver.

MATILDE. Yes, doctor.

Matilde gets out silver polish and begins polishing.
Lane watches her for a moment, then exits.

6. Matilde

Matilde stops cleaning.

MATILDE. This is how I imagine my parents.

Music.
A dashing couple appears.

MATILDE. They are dancing.
They are not the best dancers in the world.

They laugh until laughing makes them kiss.
They kiss until kissing makes them laugh.

They dance.
They laugh until laughing makes them kiss.
They kiss until kissing makes them laugh.
Matilde watches.

7. Virginia and Matilde

The doorbell rings.
The music stops.
Matilde's parents exit.
They blow kisses to Matilde.
Matilde waves back.
The doorbell rings again.
Matilde answers the door.

MATILDE. Hello.
VIRGINIA. Hello. You are the maid?
MATILDE. Yes.
You are the sister?
VIRGINIA. Yes.
How did you know?
MATILDE. I dusted your photograph.

My boss said: this is my sister.
We don't look alike.
I thought: you don't look like my boss. You must be her sister.
My name is Matilde. *(Brazilian pronunciation of Matilde.)*
VIRGINIA:. I thought your name was Matilde. *(American pronunciation of Matilde.)*
MATILDE. Kind of.
VIRGINIA. Nice to meet you.
MATILDE. Nice to meet you. I don't know your name.
VIRGINIA. Oh! My name is Virginia.
MATILDE. Like the state?
VIRGINIA. Yes.

Matilde continues to stand in front of the door.

MATILDE. I've never been to Virginia.
VIRGINIA. Maybe I should go.
MATILDE. To Virginia?
VIRGINIA. No. I mean—am I interrupting you?
MATILDE. No. I was just—cleaning. Your sister is at work.
VIRGINIA. She's always at work.
MATILDE. Would you like to come in?
VIRGINIA. Yes. Actually—I came to see you.
MATILDE. Me?
VIRGINIA. Lane tells me that you've been feeling a little blue.
MATILDE. Blue?
VIRGINIA. Sad.
MATILDE. Oh. She told you that?
VIRGINIA. Come, sit on the couch with me.
MATILDE. Okay.

Virginia goes to sit on the couch.
She pats the couch.
Matilde sits down next to her.

VIRGINIA. Do you miss home?

MATILDE. Of course I do. Doesn't everyone?

VIRGINIA. Is that why you've been sad?

MATILDE. No. I don't think so. It's just that—I don't like to clean houses. I think it makes me sad.

VIRGINIA. You don't like to clean houses.

MATILDE. No.

VIRGINIA. But that's so simple!

MATILDE. Yes.

VIRGINIA. Why don't you like to clean?

MATILDE. I've never liked to clean. When I was a child I thought: if the floor is dirty, look at the ceiling. It is always clean.

VIRGINIA. I like cleaning.

MATILDE. You do? Why?

VIRGINIA. It clears my head.

MATILDE. So it is, for you, a religious practice?

VIRGINIA. No. It's just that: cleaning my house—makes me feel clean.

MATILDE. But you don't clean other people's houses. For money.

VIRGINIA. No—I clean my own house.

MATILDE. I think that is different.

VIRGINIA. Do you feel sad *while* you are cleaning? Or before? Or after?

MATILDE. I am sad when I think about cleaning. But I try not to think about cleaning while I am cleaning. I try to think of jokes. But

sometimes the cleaning makes me mad. And then I'm not in a funny
mood. And *that* makes me sad. Would you like a coffee?
    VIRGINIA. I would *love* some coffee.

Matilde goes to get a cup of coffee from the kitchen.
Virginia puts her finger on the tabletops to test the dust.
Then she wipes her dirty finger on her skirt.
Then she tries to clean her skirt but she has nothing to clean it with.
Matilde comes back and gives her the coffee.

    VIRGINIA. Thank you.
    MATILDE. You're welcome.

Virginia drinks the coffee.

    VIRGINIA. This is good coffee.
    MATILDE. We make good coffee in Brazil.
    VIRGINIA. Oh—that's right. You do!
    MATILDE. Does that help you to place me in my cultural context?
    VIRGINIA. Lane didn't describe you accurately.
    How old are you?
    MATILDE. Young enough that my skin is still good.
    Old enough that I am starting to think: is my skin still good?
    Does that answer your question?
    VIRGINIA. Yes. You're twenty-seven.

Matilde nods.

    MATILDE. You're good.
    VIRGINIA. Thank you.

Listen. Matilde. *(American pronunciation)*
MATILDE. Matilde. *(Brazilian pronunciation.)*
VIRGINIA. Yes.
I have a proposition for you.
MATILDE. A proposition?
VIRGINIA. A deal.
I like to clean. You do not like to clean. Why don't I clean for you.
MATILDE. You're joking.
VIRGINIA. No.
MATILDE. I don't get it. What do you want from me?
VIRGINIA. Nothing.
MATILDE. Then—why?
VIRGINIA. I have my house cleaned by approximately 3:12 every afternoon. I have folded the corner of every sheet. The house is quiet. The gold draperies are singing a little lullaby to the ottoman. The silverware is gently sleeping in its box. I tuck in the forks, the spoons, the knives. I do not have children.
MATILDE. I'm sorry.
VIRGINIA. *(Faster and faster)* Don't be sorry. My husband is barren. I never thought that the world was quite good enough for children anyway. I didn't trust myself to cope with how sick and ugly the world is and how beautiful children are and the idea of watching them grow into the dirt and mess of the world—someone might kidnap them or rape them or otherwise trample on their innocence, leaving them in the middle of the road, naked, in some perverse sexual position, to die while strangers rode past on bicycles and tried not to look. I've thought about doing some volunteer work, but I don't know who to volunteer for.

A pause. She looks at Matilde.

VIRGINIA. Since I was twenty-two, my life has gone down hill, and not only have I not done what I wanted to do, but I have lost the qualities and temperament that would help me reverse the downward spiral—and now I am a completely different person.

I don't know why I am telling you all of this, Mathalina.

Matilde and Virginia look at each other.
Matilde thinks about correcting Virginia. She doesn't.

MATILDE. Go on.

VIRGINIA. I used to study Greek literature. One summer my husband and I went to Europe. It was supposed to be relaxing but I have trouble relaxing on vacations. We were going to see ruins and I was going to write about ruins but I found that I had nothing to say about them. I thought: why doesn't someone just sweep them up! Get a very large broom!

I'm sorry. I was trying to say...

MATILDE. You were telling me how your life has gone down-hill since you were twenty-two.

VIRGINIA. Yes. The point is: every day my house is cleaned by 3 o'clock. I have a lot of—time.

I'd be very happy to come here and clean Lane's house before Lane gets home from work. That is what I'm telling you. Only don't tell her. She wouldn't like it.

MATILDE. I will let you clean the house if it will make you feel better.

VIRGINIA. Let's start in the bathroom. I love cleaning the toilet. It's so dirty, and then it's so clean!

8. Lane and Matilde

Matilde is reading the funny papers.
Lane enters.

> LANE. It's so clean!
> MATILDE. Yes.
> LANE. The medication is helping?
> MATILDE. I'm feeling much better.
> LANE. Well—that's terrific.

Lane exits.
Matilde takes out her medication.
She undoes the bottle,
takes one pill out,
looks at it,
and throws it in the garbage can.

9. Matilde

Matilde, to the audience.

MATILDE. The perfect joke makes you forget about your life. The perfect joke makes you remember about your life. The perfect joke is stupid when you write it down. The perfect joke was not made up by one person. It passed through the air and you caught it. A perfect joke is somewhere between an angel and a fart.

This is how I imagine my parents:

Music.
Matilde's mother and father appear.
They sit at a cafe.

> My mother and father are at a cafe.
> My mother is telling my father a joke.
> It is a dirty joke.
> My father is laughing so hard that he is banging his knee on the underside of the table.
> My mother is laughing so hard that she spits out her coffee.
> I am with them at the cafe. I am eight years old.
> I say: what's so funny?
> (I *hate* not understanding a joke.)
> My mother says: Ask me again when you're thirty.
> Now I'm almost thirty. And I'll never know the joke.

Matilde's mother and father look at her.
They exit.

10. Virginia and Matilde

The next day.
Virginia folds laundry.
Matilde watches.
Virginia is happy to be cleaning.

MATILDE. You're good at that.
VIRGINIA. Thank you.
MATILDE. You want to hear a joke?
VIRGINIA. Not really.
MATILDE. Why?
VIRGINIA. I don't like to laugh out loud.
MATILDE. Why?
VIRGINIA. I don't like my laugh. It's like a wheeze. Someone once told me that. Who was it—my husband? Do you have a husband?
MATILDE. No.
VIRGINIA. That's good.
MATILDE. Do you like your husband?
VIRGINIA. My husband is like a well-placed couch. He takes up the right amount of space. A man should not be too beautiful. Or too good in bed. A man should be—functional. And well-chosen. Otherwise you're in trouble.
MATILDE. Does he make you laugh?
VIRGINIA. Oh, no. Something uncontrollable would come out of my mouth when he wanted it to. I wouldn't like that.
MATILDE. A good joke cleans your insides out. If I don't laugh for a week, I feel dirty. I feel dirty now, like my insides are rotting.
VIRGINIA. Someone should make you laugh. I'm not the person

to do it.

MATILDE. Virginia. My mother once said to me: Matilde, in order to tell a good joke, you have to believe that your problems are very small, and that the world is very big. She said: if more women knew more jokes, there would be more justice in this world.

Virginia starts folding underwear.
Matilde watches.

VIRGINIA. I've never seen my sister's underwear before.
MATILDE. Her underwear is practical. And white.

Virginia continues to fold underwear.

VIRGINIA. I wonder if Lane has gone through menopause yet. Her underwear *is* very white. Some women throw out underwear when they get a bloodstain. Other women keep washing the stain.
MATILDE. I can't afford to throw away underwear. If I could, believe me, I would. I would buy new underwear every day: purple, red, gold, orange, silver...

Virginia folds a pair of men's underwear.

VIRGINIA. It's a little weird to be touching my brother-in-law's underwear.

He's a very handsome man.

When he and Lane first met, I thought: Lane gets the best of everything. A surgeon. With a specialty. He's—charismatic.

Virginia touches her brother-in-laws underwear as she folds.

VIRGINIA. Then I thought: it's better to have a husband who is not *too* handsome. Then you don't worry about him.

Virginia comes across a pair of women's black underwear.

VIRGINIA. These don't look like Lane.
MATILDE. No.
VIRGINIA. Too shiny.
MATILDE. Too sexy.

Matilde and Virginia look at each other.

Mess starts here
something is go... on
VA attracted

11. Lane and Virginia Have Coffee.

Lane and Virginia have coffee in the living room.

VIRGINIA. The house is so clean!
LANE. Thanks.
VIRGINIA. It's working out—with your maid? What's her name?
LANE. *(American pronunciation.)* Matilde.
VIRGINIA. That's right. Mathilda. *(American pronunciation.)* Don't they say Matilde *(Brazilian pronunciation)* in Brazil?
LANE. I don't know.
VIRGINIA. I think they do.
LANE. How would you know?

Virginia shrugs.

VIRGINIA. Mm...

LANE. Well, I'm sure she would tell me if I were saying her name wrong. Anyway. She seems much better. How are you?

VIRGINIA. Oh, fine.

How's Charles?

LANE. Why do you ask?

VIRGINIA. No reason.

LANE. He's fine.

VIRGINIA. That's good. The last time I saw Charles was Christmas. You both work so hard.

LANE. He's been doing nine surgeries a day—we hardly see each other. I mean, of course we see each other, but, you know how it is. More coffee?

VIRGINIA. No, thanks.

LANE. Matilde! Could you clear these, please?

Matilde enters from the kitchen.

MATILDE: *(to Virginia)* Your cup, miss?

VIRGINIA. Oh, I'll get it—

Matilde winks at Virginia.
Matilde clears the plates.

VIRGINIA. Thanks.

MATILDE. Did everyone enjoy their coffee?

LANE and VIRGINIA. Yes.

MATILDE. Good.

She exits.

LANE. Oh. That's Matilde. Sorry. That was rude. I should have introduced you. Or is it rude? Do you introduce the maid to the company?

VIRGINIA. I'm not the company. I'm your sister.

LANE. You're right.

I should have introduced you. I can't get used to having another person in the house.

VIRGINIA. Mmm. Yes. It must make you uncomfortable to—I don't know—read a magazine while someone cleans up after you.

LANE. I don't read magazines, Virginia. I go to work exhausted and I come home exhausted. That is how most of the people in this country function. At least people who have jobs.

A pause.
For a moment,
Lane and Virginia experience
a primal moment during which they
are seven and nine years old,
inside the mind, respectively.
They are mad.
Then they return quite naturally
to language, as adults do.

LANE. Sorry—I didn't mean—
VIRGINIA. I know.

At the same time:

VIRGINIA. Are you—?   LANE. I keep meaning to—

VIRGINIA. What?

LANE. Oh—it's just—I keep meaning to have you two over for dinner. It's ridiculous—living so close and never seeing each other.

VIRGINIA. You're right. Maybe next week?

LANE. Next week is crazy. But soon.

Virginia nods.

12. Lane and Matilde

Night.
Matilde tries to think up the perfect joke.
Matilde looks straight ahead,
in the dark, in the living room.
She thinks.
Lane comes home from work.
She turns a light on.

LANE. Oh! You startled me.

MATILDE. You startled me too.

LANE. What are you doing in the dark?

MATILDE. I was trying to think up a joke.
I almost had one.
Now it's gone.

LANE. Oh—well—can you get it back again?
MATILDE. I doubt it.
LANE. Oh.
Is Charles home?
MATILDE. No.
LANE. Did he call?
MATILDE. No.
LANE. Oh, well, he's probably just sleeping at the hospital.

Matilde is silent.

LANE. Sometimes there's no time to call home from the hospital. You're going from patient to patient, and it's—you know—crazy. When we were younger—Charles and I—if we had a crazy night at the hospital—we would page each other, we had this signal—two for good-night—and three for—well, I don't know why I'm thinking about this right now. The point is—when you get older, you just *know* that a person is thinking of you, and working hard, and thinking of you, and you don't need them to call anymore. Since Charles and I are both doctors we both—understand—how it is.
MATILDE. Mmm.

A silence.

LANE. Well, good-night.
MATILDE. Good-night.
LANE. Are you going to—just—sit here in the dark?
MATILDE. I might stay up a little longer to—what's the word?—tidy up.
LANE. Oh. Great. Just shut the light off when you—

Matilde turns the light off.

> LANE. Oh. Good-night.
> MATILDE. Good-night.

Lane exits.
Matilde tries to think up the perfect joke.
Matilde closes her eyes.
Night turns to day.

13. Virginia and Matilde. Then Lane.

Virginia irons.
Matilde watches.

> MATILDE. I have a really good joke coming.
> VIRGINIA. That's good.
> MATILDE. You know how most jokes go in threes? Like this: Da da DA. I'm making up one that goes in sixes: Da da Da da da DA.
> VIRGINIA. I didn't know jokes had time signatures.
> MATILDE. Oh, they do. Ask me what my profession is then ask me what my greatest problem is.
> VIRGINIA. What's your profession?
> MATILDE. I'm a comedian.
> VIRGINIA. What's your—
> MATILDE. Timing.

VIRGINIA. That's good.

MATILDE. But you're not laughing.

VIRGINIA. I'm laughing on the inside.

MATILDE. Oh. I like it better when people laugh on the outside. I'm looking for the perfect joke, but I'm afraid if I found it, it would kill me.

Virginia comes upon a pair of women's red underwear.

VIRGINIA. My God!

MATILDE. Oh...

No— *(as in—he wouldn't dare)*

VIRGINIA. No.

MATILDE. But— *(as in—he might dare)*

VIRGINIA. Do you think—here—in the house?

MATILDE. Maybe a park. I bet he puts them in his pocket, afterwards, and forgets, because he's so happy. And then she's walking around for the day, with no underwear, and you know what? She probably likes it.

VIRGINIA. I hope it's not a nurse. It's such a cliché.

MATILDE. If she's a nurse, they would pass each other in the hospital, and she would say, hello doctor. And she knows, and he knows: no underwear.

VIRGINIA. No underwear in a *hospital?* It's unsanitary.

MATILDE. Or—maybe he just *likes* women's underwear. He might try them on.

VIRGINIA. Charles? No!

MATILDE. It's possible. You don't like to think about it, because he's your brother-in-law, but these things happen, Virginia. They do.

Lane enters.
Virginia quickly puts down the iron and sits down.
Matilde stands and begins to iron.
Virginia hides the red underwear.

LANE. *(to Virginia)* What are you doing here?
VIRGINIA. Nothing. How was work?

Lane doesn't say anything.
She moves to the kitchen.

VIRGINIA. Where are you going?
LANE. I'm going in the other room to shoot myself.
VIRGINIA. You're joking, right?
LANE. *(from the kitchen)* Right.

Matilde and Virginia look at each other.
Matilde irons underwear.
Virginia sits.
Virginia stands.   *nervous*
Virginia sits.
Virginia stands.
Virginia has a deep impulse to order the universe.   *cleaning*
Virginia arranges objects on the coffee table.   *stress*
Lane enters.
Her left hand is bleeding.
She holds it with a dish towel.

VIRGINIA. Lane—what—are you—?
LANE. I'm disguising myself as a patient.

VIRGINIA. That's not funny.
LANE. I cut myself.

They look at her, alarmed.

LANE. Don't worry. Even my wounds are superficial.
VIRGINIA. Lane?
LANE. Can opener. I was making a martini.
VIRGINIA. Why do you need a can opener to make a martini?
LANE. I didn't have the right kind of fucking olives, okay? I only have black olives! In a can.
VIRGINIA. Lane?
LANE. He's gone off with a patient.
VIRGINIA. What?
LANE. His patient.
MATILDE. Oh...
LANE. Yes.

Virginia and Matilde glance towards the underwear and look away.

VIRGINIA. Was it a—?
LANE. Mastectomy. Yes.
VIRGINIA. Wow. That's very—
LANE. Generous of him?
MATILDE. A mastectomy?

Virginia gestures towards her breast.
Matilde nods.

VIRGINIA. How old is she?

LANE. Sixty-seven.
VIRGINIA and MATILDE. Oh!
LANE. What?
VIRGINIA. Not what I expected.
LANE. A young nurse? The maid? No. He's in love.
VIRGINIA. But—with an older woman?
LANE. Yes.
VIRGINIA. I'm almost—impressed. She must have—substance.
LANE. She's not a doctor.
VIRGINIA. Well, most men in his position...he's still—so—good-looking...
LANE. Virginia!
VIRGINIA. Sorry.
LANE. I've never been jealous, I've never been suspicious. I've never thought any other woman was my equal. I'm the best doctor. I'm the smartest, the most well-loved by my patients. I'm athletic. I have poise. I've aged well. I can talk to *anyone* and be on equal footing. How, I thought, could he even *look* at anyone else. It would be absurd.
VIRGINIA. Wow. You really are—confident.
LANE. I was blind. He didn't want a doctor. He wanted a housewife.

A pause.
Matilde irons.
Lane looks around the house.
She sees the objects on the coffee-table—
a vase, some magazines, forcefully arranged.

LANE. *(to Virginia)* Have you been cleaning my house?

Virginia and Matilde look at each other.

VIRGINIA. No, I haven't been cleaning your house.
LANE. These objects on the coffee table—that is how you arrange objects.

Virginia looks at the coffee table.

VIRGINIA. I don't know what you mean.
LANE. Matilde—has Virginia been cleaning the house?
VIRGINIA. I said no.
LANE. I asked Matilde.
Has Virginia been cleaning the house?
MATILDE. Yes.
LANE. For how long?
MATILDE. Two weeks.
LANE. You're fired.
You're both fired.
VIRGINIA. You can't do that.
This is my fault.
LANE. I'm *paying* her to clean my house!
VIRGINIA. And your house is clean!
LANE. This has nothing to do with you, Virginia.
VIRGINIA. This has *everything* to do with me.
LANE. Matilde—do you have enough money saved for a plane ticket back home?
MATILDE. No.
LANE. You can stay one more week. I will buy you a plane ticket.
VIRGINIA. Lane. Your husband left you today.

LANE. I'm aware of that.

VIRGINIA. You're not capable of making a rational decision.

LANE. I'm always capable of making a rational decision!

MATILDE. You don't need to buy me a plane ticket. I'm moving to New York, to become a comedian. I only need a bus ticket.

VIRGINIA: *(to LANE)* You can't do this!

LANE. I will not have you cleaning my house, just because the maid is depressed—

VIRGINIA. She's not depressed. She doesn't like to clean! It makes her sad.

Lane looks at Matilde.

LANE. Is that true?

MATILDE. Yes.

LANE. So—

then—

(to Virginia) why?

VIRGINIA. I don't know.

LANE. You looked through my things.

VIRGINIA. Not really.

LANE. I find this—incomprehensible.

VIRGINIA. Can't I do a nice thing for you without having a *motive?*

LANE. No.

VIRGINIA. That's—

LANE. You have better things to do than clean my house.

VIRGINIA. Like what?

LANE. I—

VIRGINIA. Like what?

LANE. I don't know.

VIRGINIA. No, you don't know.

I wake up in the morning, and I wish that I could sleep through the whole day because it is too painful, but there I am, I'm awake.

So I get out of bed. I make eggs for my husband. I throw the eggshells in the disposal. I listen to the sound of delicate eggshells being ground by an indelicate machine. I clean the sink. I sweep the floor. I wipe coffee grounds from the counter.

I might have done something different with my life. I might have been a scholar. I might have described one particular ruin with the cold-blooded poetry of which only a first-rate scholar is capable. Why didn't I?

LANE. I don't know.

VIRGINIA. I wanted something—big. I didn't know how to ask for it.

Don't blame Matilde. Blame me. I wanted—a task.

LANE. I'm sorry. I don't know what to say.

Except:

(to Matilde) you're fired.

VIRGINIA. It's not her fault! You can't do this.

LANE. *(to Virginia)* What would you like me to do?

VIRGINIA. Let me...take care of you.

LANE. I don't need to be taken care of.

VIRGINIA. Everybody needs to be taken care of.

LANE. Virginia. I'm all grown up. I DO NOT WANT TO BE TAKEN CARE OF.

VIRGINIA. WHY NOT?

LANE. I don't want my sister to clean my house. I want a stranger to clean my house.

Virginia and Lane look at Matilde.

MATILDE. It's all right. I'll go.
I'll pack my things.
Good-bye Virginia.
Good luck finding a task.

She embraces Virginia.

MATILDE. Good-bye, doctor.
Good luck finding your husband.

She exits.
Lane and Virginia look at each other.

14. Lane. Then Matilde. Then Virginia.

LANE. *(to the audience.)* This is how I imagine my husband and his new wife.

Charles and Ana appear.
Charles undoes Ana's gown.
Is it a hospital gown or a ball gown?

LANE. My husband undoes her gown.
He is very gentle.
He kisses her right breast.

Charles kisses Ana's right breast.

    LANE. He kisses the side of it.
    He kisses the shadow.
    He kisses her left torso.

He kisses her left torso.

    LANE. He kisses the scar,
    the one he made. *(He kisses the scar.)*
    It's a good scar.
    He's a good surgeon.
    He kisses her mouth.
    He kisses her forehead.
    It's a sacred ritual, and
    I hate him.
Matilde enters with her suitcase.
The lovers remain.
They continue to kiss one another
on different body parts, a ritual.

    MATILDE. Is there anything else before I go?
    LANE. No. Thank you.
    MATILDE. Who are they?
    LANE. My husband and the woman he loves. Don't worry. It's only my imagination.
    MATILDE. They look happy.
    LANE. Yes.
    MATILDE. People imagine that people who are in love are happy.

LANE. Yes.

MATILDE. That is why, in your country, people kill themselves on Valentine's Day.

LANE. Yes.

Charles and Ana disappear.

MATILDE. Love isn't clean like that. It's dirty. Like a good joke. Do you want to hear a joke?

LANE. Sure.

Matilde tells a joke in Portuguese. *

LANE. Is that the end?

MATILDE. Yes.

LANE. Was it funny?

MATILDE. Yes. It's not funny in translation.

LANE. I suppose I should laugh then.

MATILDE. Yes.

Lane tries to laugh.
She cries.

MATILDE. You're crying.

LANE. No, I'm not.

MATILDE. I think that you're crying.

LANE. Well—yes. I think I am.

Lane cries.
She laughs.

*See page 89 of the Production Notes

She cries.
And this goes on for some time.

Virginia enters.

VIRGINIA. Charles is at the door.
LANE. What?
VIRGINIA. Charles. In the hall.
MATILDE. Oh...
LANE. You let him in?
VIRGINIA. What could I do? And—there's a woman with him.
LANE. In the *house*?
VIRGINIA. Yes.
LANE. What does she look like?
Is she pretty?
VIRGINIA. No.
(with apology) She's beautiful.
LANE. Oh.
CHARLES. *(from off stage)* Lane?

The women turn to look at each other.
Blackout.

Intermission

ACT TWO

The white living room has become a hospital.
Or the idea of a hospital.
There is a balcony above the white living room.

1. Charles Performs Surgery on the Woman He Loves.

out of love?

Ana lies under a sheet.
Beautiful music.
A subtitle flashes:
Charles Performs Surgery on the Woman He Loves.

Charles takes out surgical equipment.
He does surgery on Ana.
It is an act of love.
If the actor who plays Charles is a good singer,
it would be nice if he could sing
an ethereal medieval love song in Latin   *HIPPA?*
about being medically cured by love.
He sings acapella as he does the surgery.
If the actress who plays Ana is a good singer,   *medical*
it would be nice if she recovered from the surgery *malpractice?*
and slowly sat up and sang a contrapuntal melody.
When the surgery is over,
Charles takes off Ana's sheet.

41

Underneath the sheet,
she is dressed in a lovely dress.
They kiss.

2. Ana

Ana, to the audience.

ANA. I have avoided doctors my whole life.

I don't like how they smell. I don't like how they talk. I don't admire their emotional lives. I don't like how they walk. They walk very fast to get somewhere—tac tac tac—I am walking somewhere important. I don't like that. I like a man who saunters. Like this.

Ana saunters across the stage like a man.

ANNA. But with Charles, it was like: BLAM!

My mind was going: you're a doctor, I hate you.

But the rest of me was gone, walking out the door, with him.

When he performed surgery on me,

we were already in love.

I was under general anesthetic but I could sense him there.

I think he put something extra in—during the surgery.

Into the missing place.

There are stories of surgeons who leave things inside the body by mistake:

[handwritten: true love overcomes many barriers]

rubber gloves, sponges, clamps—
But–you know—I think Charles left his soul inside me.
Into the missing place.

She touches her left breast.

3. Charles

Charles, to the audience.

CHARLES. There are jokes about breast surgeons.
You know—something like—I've seen more breasts in this city than—
I don't know the punch line.
There must be a punch line.
I'm not a man who falls in love easily. I've been faithful to my wife. We fell in love when we were twenty-two. We had plans. There was justice in the world. There was justice in love. If a person was good enough, an equally good person would fall in love with that person. And then I met—Ana. Justice had nothing to do with it.
There once was a very great American surgeon named Halsted. He was married to a nurse. He loved her—immeasurably. One day Halsted noticed that his wife's hands were chapped and red when she came back from surgery. And so he invented rubber gloves. For her. It is one of the great love stories in medicine. The difference between inspired medicine and uninspired medicine is love.

[handwritten: justify w/ example
surgeon not cheating
to slightly cheating
fall in love so long, not that bad]

When I met Ana, I knew:
I loved her to the point of invention.

4. Charles and Ana

CHARLES. I'm afraid that you have breast cancer.

ANA. If you think I'm going to cry, I'm not going to cry.

CHARLES. It's normal to cry—

ANA. I don't cry when I'm supposed to cry.

Are you going to cut it off?

CHARLES. You must need some time—to digest—

ANA. No. I don't need time. Tell me everything.

CHARLES. You have a variety of options. Many women don't opt for a mastectomy. A lumpectomy and radiation can be just as effective as—

ANA. I want you to cut it off.

CHARLES. You might want to talk with family members—with a husband—are you married?—or with—

ANA. Tomorrow.

CHARLES. Tomorrow?

ANA. Tomorrow.

CHARLES. I'm not sure I have any appointments open tomorrow—

ANA. I'd like you to do it tomorrow.

CHARLES. Then we'll do it tomorrow.

They look at each other.

They fall in love.

ANA. Then I'll see you tomorrow, at the surgery.
CHARLES. Good-bye, Ana.
ANA. Good-bye.

They look at each other.
They fall in love some more.
She turns to go. She turns back.

ANA. Am I going to die?
CHARLES. No. You're not going to die.
I won't let you die.

They fall in love completely.
They kiss wildly.

CHARLES. What's happening?
ANA. I don't know.
CHARLES. This doesn't happen to me.
ANA. Me neither.
CHARLES. Ana, Ana, Ana, Ana...your name goes backwards
and forwards.... I love you...
ANA. And I love you.
Take off your white coat.

They kiss.

5. Lane, Virginia, Matilde, Charles, and Ana

We are back in the white living room.
We are deposited at the end of the last scene from the first act.
Charles is at the door, with Ana.

CHARLES. Lane?
LANE. Charles.
CHARLES. Lane. I want us all to know each other. I want to do things right, from the beginning. Lane: this is Ana. Ana, this is my wife, Lane.
ANA. Nice to meet you. I've heard wonderful things about you. I've heard that you are a wonderful doctor.
LANE. Thank you.

Ana holds out her hand to Lane.
Lane looks around in disbelief.
Then Lane shakes Ana's hand.

CHARLES. This is my sister-in-law, Virginia.
ANA. Hello.
VIRGINIA. How do you do.
MATILDE. You look like my mother.
LANE. *(to Ana)* This is the maid. Matilde.
(to Charles) I fired her this morning.
ANA. Encantada, Matilde. *(Nice to meet you, Matilde.)*
MATILDE. Encantada. Sou do Brasil. *(Nice to meet you. I'm from Brazil.)*
ANA. Eu falo um pouco de portugues, mas que eu falo, falo

mal. *(I know a little bit of Portuguese, but it's bad.)*

MATILDE. Eh! boa tentativa! 'ta chegando la! *(Ah! Good try! Not bad.)*

Es usted de Argentina? *(You're from Argentina?)*

ANA. ¿Cómo lo sabe? *(How did you know?)*

MATILDE: *(imitating Ana's accent)* ¿Cómo lo sabe? *(How did you know?)*

They laugh.

LANE. We've all met. You can leave now, Charles.

CHARLES. What happened to your wrist?

LANE. Can opener.

CHARLES. Oh.

Charles examines the bandage on Lane's wrist.
She pulls her hand away.

MATILDE. ¿Ha usted estado alguna vez en Brasil? *(Have you ever been to Brazil?)*

ANA. Una vez, para estudiar rocas. *(Once to study rocks, in Spanish.)*

MATILDE. Rocas?

ANA. Sí, rocas.

MATILDE. Ah, rochas! *(Ah, rocks! in Portuguese, pronounced "hochas.")*

ANA. Sí!

They laugh.

VIRGINIA. Should we sit down?

They all sit down.

LANE. Virginia!—Could you get us something to drink.
VIRGINIA. What would you like?
MATILDE. I would like a coffee.
ANA. That sounds nice. I'll have coffee too.
VIRGINIA. Charles?
CHARLES. Nothing for me, thanks.
VIRGINIA. Lane?
LANE. I would like some hard alcohol in a glass with ice. Thank you.

Virginia exits.

LANE. So.
CHARLES. Lane. I know this is unorthodox. But I want us to know each other.
ANA. You are very generous to have me in your home.
LANE. Not at all.
ANA. Yes, you are very generous. I wanted to meet you. I am not a home-wrecker. The last time I fell in love it was with my husband, a long time ago. He was a geologist and a very wild man, an alcoholic. But so fun! So crazy! He peed on lawns and did everything bad and I loved it. But I did not want to have children with him because he was too wild, too crazy. I said you have to stop drinking and then he did stop drinking and then he died of cancer when he was thirty-one.

Matilde murmurs with sympathy.

ANA. My heart was broken and I said to myself: I will never love again. And I didn't. I thought I was going to meet my husband—eventually—in some kind of afterlife with fabulous rocks. Blue and green rocks. And then I met Charles. When Charles said he was married I said Charles we should stop but then Charles referred to Jewish law and I had to say that I agreed and that was that. I wanted you to understand.

LANE. Well, I don't understand. What about Jewish law.

CHARLES. In Jewish law you are legally obligated to break off relations with your wife or husband if you find what is called your *bashert.*

ANA. Your soul mate.

CHARLES. You are _obligated_ to do this. Legally bound. There's something—metaphysically—objective about it.

LANE. You're not Jewish.

CHARLES. I know. But I heard about the *bashert*—on a radio program. And it always stuck with me. When I saw Ana I knew that was it. I knew she was my bashert.

ANA. There is a *midrash* that says when a baby is forty days old, inside the mother's stomach, God picks out its soul mate, and people have to spend the rest of their lives running around to find each other.

CHARLES. Lane. Something very objective happened to me. It's as though I suddenly tested positive for a genetic disease that I've had all along. *Ana has been in my genetic code.*

ANA. Yes. It is strange. We didn't feel guilty because it was so *objective.* And yet both of us are moral people. I don't know Charles very well but I think he is moral but to tell you the truth even if he were immoral I would love him because the love I feel for your husband is so overpowering.

LANE. And this is what you've come to tell me. That you're both

innocent according to Jewish law.
ANA and CHARLES. Yes.

Virginia enters with the drinks.

MATILDE. Thank you.

Lane takes the glass from Virginia.

LANE. *(to Virginia)* Charles has come to tell me that according to Jewish law, he has found his soul mate, and so our marriage is dissolved. He doesn't even need to feel guilty. How about that.
VIRGINIA. You have found your *bashert.*
LANE. How the hell do you know about a *bashert?*
VIRGINIA. I heard it on public radio.
CHARLES. I'm sorry that it happened to you, Lane. It could just as well have happened the other way. You might have met your *bashert*, and I would have been forced to make way. There are things—big invisible things—that come unannounced—they walk in, and we have to give way. I would even congratulate you. Because I have always loved you.
LANE. Well. Congratulations.

A silence. A cold one.

MATILDE. Would anyone like to hear a joke?
ANA. I would.

Matilde tells a joke in Portuguese.*
Ana laughs. No one else laughs.

ANA. ¡Qué bueno! ¡Qué chiste más bueno! *(What a good joke!)*
(to Lane) You are firing Matilde?

LANE. Yes.

ANA. Then we'll hire her to clean our house. I hate to clean. And Charles likes things to be clean. At least I think he does. Charles? Do you like things to be clean?

CHARLES. Sure. I like things to be clean.

ANA. Matilde? Would you like to work for us?

MATILDE. There is something you should know. I don't like to clean so much.

ANA. Of course you don't. Do you have any other skills?

MATILDE. I can tell jokes.

ANA. Perfect. She's coming to live with us.

LANE. My God! You can't just walk into my home and take everything away from me.

ANA. I thought you fired this young woman.

LANE. Yes. I did.

ANA. Have you changed your mind?

LANE. I don't know. Maybe.

ANA. Matilde, do you have a place to live?

MATILDE. No.

ANA. So she'll come live with us.

VIRGINIA. Matilde is like family.

MATILDE. What?

VIRGINIA. Matilde is like a sister to me.

ANA. Is this true?

MATILDE. I don't know. I never had a sister.

VIRGINIA. We clean together. We talk, and fold laundry, as women used to do. They would gather at the public fountains and wash their clothes and tell stories. Now we are alone in our separate

*See page 95 of the Production Notes

houses and it is terrible.

ANA So it is Virginia who wants you to stay. Not Lane.

LANE. We both want her to stay. We love Matilde. *(an attempt at the Brazilian pronunciation of Matilde.)*

ANA. Matilde?

MATILDE. I am confused.

LANE. I depend on Matilde. I couldn't stand to replace her. Matilde—are you unhappy here with us?

MATILDE. I—

LANE. Is it the money? You could have a raise.

ANA. Matilde—you should do as you wish. My house is easy to clean. I own hardly anything. I own one table, two chairs, a bed, one painting and I have a little fish whose water needs to be changed. I don't have rugs so there is no vacuuming. But you would have to do Charles' laundry. I will not be his washerwoman.

VIRGINIA. Excuse me. But I think that people who are in love— really in love—would like to clean up after each other. If I were in love with Charles I would enjoy folding his laundry.

Virginia looks at Charles.
Lane looks at Virginia.

ANA. Matilde—what do you think? Would you like to work for us?

VIRGINIA. Please don't leave us, Matilde.

MATILDE. I will split my time. Half with Lane and Virginia, half with Ana and Charles. How is that?

ANA. Lane?

LANE. Matilde is a free agent.

ANA. Of course she is.

CHARLES. Well.

That's settled.
LANE. Are you leaving now?
CHARLES. Do you want me to leave?

A pause.

LANE. Yes.
CHARLES. Okay. Then we'll leave.
Ana and I are going apple picking this afternoon.
She's never been apple picking.
Would anyone like to join us?
MATILDE. I've never been apple picking.
CHARLES. So Matilde will come. Virginia?
VIRGINIA. I love apple picking.
LANE. Virginia!
CHARLES. Lane?
LANE. You must be insane! Apple picking! My god! I'M
SORRY! But—apple picking? This is not a foreign film! We don't
have an *arrangement!* You don't even *like* foreign films! Maybe
you'll pretend to like foreign films, for *Ana*, but I can tell you now
Ana, he doesn't like them! He doesn't like reading the little subtitles!
It gives him a headache!
CHARLES. Lane. I don't expect you to—understand this—
immediately. But since this thing—has happened to me—I want to
live life to the fullest. I know—what it must sound like. But it's different. I want to go apple picking. I want to go to Machu Picchu. You
can be part of that. I want to share my happiness with you.
LANE. I don't want your happiness.
MATILDE. *(to Ana)* Es cómo una telenovela. *(It's like a soap
opera.)*

Tan triste. *(So sad.)*
CHARLES. Lane—I—
LANE. What.
CHARLES. I hope that you'll forgive me one day.
LANE. Go pick some apples.
Good-bye.
CHARLES. Good-bye.
ANA. Good-bye.
MATILDE. Good-bye.
VIRGINIA. I'll stay.

Ana, Matilde, and Charles exit.

LANE. I want to be alone.
VIRGINIA. No, you don't.
LANE. Yes, I do.
VIRGINIA. No, you don't.

Lane sits on the couch.
Virginia pats her shoulder, awkward.

VIRGINIA. Do you want—I don't know—a hot water bottle?
LANE. No, I don't want a hot water bottle, Virginia.
VIRGINIA. I just thought—
LANE. —That I'm nine years old with a cold?
VIRGINIA. I don't know what else to do.

A pause.

LANE. You know, actually, I think I'd like one. It sounds nice.

6. Ana and Matilde. Then Charles.

Ana and Matilde are up on Ana's balcony.
It is high above the white living room.
It is a small perch, overlooking the sea.
Through French doors,
one can enter or exit the balcony.
A room leading to the balcony is suggested but unseen.
Matilde and Ana wear sunglasses and sunhats.
They are surrounded by apples.

Underneath the balcony,
Lane is in her living room.
She lies down with a hot water bottle.

Ana polishes an apple.
They look around at all of the apples.

ANA. Nunca nos vamos a comer todas estas malditas manzanas.
(We're never going to eat all of these damn apples.)*

MATILDE. Mas é legal ter um monte. *(But it's nice to have so many.)*

Tantas que é uma loucura ter tantas assim. *(So many that it's crazy to have so many.)*

Porque você nunca pode comer todas elas. *(Because you can never eat them all.)*

---

*According to the actor's linguistic abilities, this scene may be spoken in English if necessary. If spoken in Spanish and Portuguese, the director may choose to use English subtitles.

ANA. Si.

Ana picks out an apple and eats it.

MATILDE. Eu gusto das verdes. *(I like the green ones.)*
De quais você gosta? *(Which ones do you like?)*

ANA. Las amarillas. Son más dulces. *(The yellow ones. They're sweeter.)*

MATILDE. We could take one bite of each and if it's not a really, really good apple we can throw it into the sea.

ANA. Ahora vos estás hablando como una Norte Americana. *(Now you're talking like a North American.)*

MATILDE. Vai ser engraçado. *(It will be fun.)*

ANA. Okay.

They start taking bites of each apple
and if they don't think it's a perfect apple
they throw it into the sea.
The sea is also Lane's living room.
Lane sees the apples fall into her living room.
She looks at them.

MATILDE. Eu inventei uma piada nova hoje. *(I made up a new joke today.)*

ANA. Ah! Bueno!

MATILDE. I made up eighty-four new jokes since I started working for you. I only made up one at the other house. Mas era uma boa. *(It was a good one though.)* Sometimes you have to suffer for the really good ones.

ANA. Why don't you tell jokes for a job?

MATILDE. Algum dia. *(Someday.)*

Matilde throws an apple core into the living room.

ANA. Por qué algun día? Por qué no ahora? *(Why someday? Why not now?)*

MATILDE. I'm looking for the perfect joke. But I am afraid if I found it, it would kill me.

ANA. Por qué? *(Why?)*

MATILDE. Minha mãe morreu rindo. *(My mother died laughing.)*

ANA. Lo siento. *(I'm sorry.)*

MATILDE. Obrigada. *(Thank you.)*

She was laughing at one of my father's jokes.

ANA. What was the joke?

MATILDE. Eu nunca vou saber. *(I'll never know.)* Let's not talk about sad things.

Matilde finds a really really good apple.

MATILDE. Prove essa. *(Try this one.)*

Matilde tries it.

ANA. Mmmm. Perfecta.

CHARLES. *(From off stage:)* Ana!

ANA. We're on the balcony!

Charles rushes in wearing scrubs and carrying an enormous bouquet of flowers. He goes to Ana and kisses her all over and continues to kiss her all over.

>ANA. My love!
>We were just eating apples.
>CHARLES. Aren't they delicious?
>ANA. Here is the very best one.

Charles takes a bite of the best apple.

>CHARLES. Divine!
>Excuse me, Matilde.
>I need to borrow this woman.

He kisses Ana.
He picks up Ana and carries her off into the bedroom.

>MATILDE. Have fun.
>ANA and CHARLES. Thank you! We will!

They exit.

>MATILDE:(*to the audience*)
>The perfect joke happens by accident. The perfect joke is the perfect music. You want to hear it only once in your life, and then, never again.

A subtitle projects:
Matilde tries to think up the perfect joke.
She looks out at the sea.
She thinks.

7. Matilde, Virginia and Lane

Virginia is cleaning.
Lane shuffles cards.

LANE: *(Shouting to Matilde who is off-stage.)*
Matilde! Your deal.

Matilde leaves the balcony.
Lane shuffles the cards.

VIRGINIA. Lane—your couch is filthy. Wouldn't it be nice to have a fresh clean slip-cover? I could sew you one.
LANE. That would be nice. It would give you a project.

Matilde enters.

LANE. Your deal.

Matilde sits.
Above them, on the balcony,
Ana and Charles dance a slow dance.

LANE. So.
Are you happy there? At the other house?
MATILDE. Yes.
LANE. What's her house like?
MATILDE. It's little. She has a balcony that overlooks the sea.
LANE. What's her furniture like?

MATILDE. A table from one place—a chair from another place. It doesn't go together. But it's nice.

LANE. What does she cook?

MATILDE. I'm not a spy!

LANE. I'm sorry.

They play cards.
On the balcony,
Charles and Ana finish their dance.
They exit, into the bedroom.
Lane puts down a card.

LANE. Do they seem like they are very much in love?

MATILDE. Yes—they are very in love.

LANE. How can you—tell?

MATILDE. They stay in bed half the day. Charles doesn't go to work. He cancels half his patients. He wants to spend all his time with Ana.

LANE. Oh.

A pause.

MATILDE. Because Ana is dying again.

LANE. What?

MATILDE. Her disease came back.

She says she won't take any medicine.

She says it's poison.

He says:

CHARLES. *(from the balcony)* You have to go to the hospital!

MATILDE. And she says:

ANA. *(from the balcony)* I won't go to the hospital!
MATILDE. Then they really fight.
It's like a soap opera.
Charles yells and throws things at the wall.
LANE. Charles never yells.
MATILDE. Oh, he yells.
And Ana yells and throws things at him.
They broke all the condiments and spices yesterday.
There was this yellow spice—
and it got in their hair and on their faces
until they were all yellow.

From the balcony:

ANA. I don't want a doctor!
I want a man!
NO HOSPITALS!

A spice jar goes flying.
A cloud of yellow spice lands in Lane's living room.

LANE. She won't go to the hospital?
MATILDE. No.
I might have to spend more time—you know—at the other house.
To help.
VIRGINIA. Poor Charles.
LANE. Poor Charles?
Poor Ana.
Poor me!
Poor sounds funny if you say it lots of times in a row: poor poor

poor poor poor. Poor. Poor. Poor. Doesn't it sound funny?
    VIRGINIA. Lane? Are you all right?
    LANE. Oh, me? I'm fine.

8. Ana and Charles. Then, Matilde.

Ana and Charles sit on the balcony.
Ana is dressed in a bathrobe.
Ana and Charles try to read one another's mind.
Below the balcony, in the living room,
Lane and Virginia fold laundry together.

    CHARLES. Eight.
    ANA. No, seven. You were very close.
    CHARLES. I'll go again.
    ANA. Okay.
    CHARLES. Four.
    ANA. Yes!
    CHARLES. I knew it! I could see four apples. Now, colors.
    ANA. Okay.
    CHARLES. I'll start.
    ANA. Red.
    CHARLES. No.
    ANA. Blue.
    CHARLES. No.
    ANA. I give up.

CHARLES. Purple.
We have to concentrate harder. Like this. Ready? You go.
ANA. I'm tired.
CHARLES. I'm sorry. I'll stop.

Charles rubs Ana's head.

ANA. Why all these guessing games?
CHARLES. You know Houdini?
ANA. The magician?
CHARLES. Yes. Houdini and his wife practiced reading each other's minds. So that—if one of them died—they'd be able to talk to each other—you know, after.
ANA. Did it work?
CHARLES. No.
ANA. Oh.
CHARLES. But I love you more than Houdini loved his wife. He was distracted—by his magic. I'm not distracted. Ana. Let's go to the hospital.
ANA. I told you.
No hospitals!

Charles makes a strange sad animal sound.

ANA. Don't be sad, Charles.
CHARLES. Don't be sad! My God!
ANA. I can't take this.
I'm going for a swim.
Matilde!
Come look after Charles.

I'm going swimming.

Ana exits.
Charles looks out over the balcony,
watching Ana run out to the water.

CHARLES. *(to Ana)* Ana! Think of a country under the water!
I'll guess it from the balcony!
MATILDE. She can't hear you.

Charles disrobes to his underwear.
He throws his clothes into Lane's living room.

CHARLES. Excuse me, Matilde. I'm going for a swim.
MATILDA. I thought you can't swim.
CHARLES. I'll learn to swim.

Underneath the balcony, in Lane's living room,
Lane comes across Charles' sweater.
She breathes it in.
She weeps.
Charles finishes disrobing and leans over the balcony.

CHARLES. Ana! What's the country? I think it's a very small
country! Is it Luxembourg? Ana!

He runs off.
Matilde looks out over the water.
A pause.
Matilde is startled.

Suddenly, with great clarity,
Matilde thinks up the perfect joke.

>   MATILDE. My God.
>   Oh no.
>   My God.
>   It's the perfect joke.
>   Am I dead?
>   No.

9. Lane, Virginia. Then Matilde.

Lane sits with Charles' sweater in her hands.
Virginia enters, vacuuming.

>   LANE. Stop it!
>   VIRGINIA. What?
>   LANE. Stop cleaning!
>   VIRGINIA. Why?
>   LANE. *(over the vacuum)* I DON'T WANT ANYTHING IN MY
> HOUSE TO BE CLEAN EVER AGAIN! I WANT THERE TO BE
> DIRT AND PIGS IN THE CORNER AND LOTS OF DIRTY FUCK-
> ING SOCKS—AND NONE OF THEM MATCH—NONE OF
> THEM—BECAUSE YOU KNOW WHAT—THAT IS HOW I FEEL
>   .

Lane unplugs the vacuum.

VIRGINIA. Wow. I'm sorry.

LANE. AND YOU KNOW WHAT? I WILL NOT LET MY HOUSE BE A BREEDING GROUND FOR YOUR WEIRD OBSESSIVE DIRT FETISH. I WILL NOT PERMIT YOU TO FEEL LIKE A BETTER PERSON JUST BECAUSE YOU PUSH DIRT AROUND ALL DAY ON MY BEHALF.

VIRGINIA. I was just trying to help.

LANE. Well, it's not helping.

VIRGINIA. I wonder—when it was—that you became—such a bitch? Oh, yes, I remember. Since the day you were born, you thought that anyone with a *problem* had a defect of the will. Well, you know what? You're wrong about that. Some people have problems, real problems—

LANE. Yes. I see people with *real problems* all day long. At the hospital.

VIRGINIA. I think—there's a small part of me—that's enjoyed watching your life fall apart. To see you lose your composure. For once. I thought--we could be sisters. Real sisters who tell each other real things. But I was wrong. Well, fine. I'm not picking up your dry cleaning anymore. I'm going to get a job.

LANE. What job?

VIRGINIA. Any job!

LANE. What are you qualified to do at this point?

VIRGINIA. No wonder Charles left. You have no compassion.

Overlapping:

LANE.	VIRGINIA.
I do so have compassion.	Ana is a woman with compassion.
I do so have compassion!	

VIRGINIA. Really. How so.

LANE. I traded my whole life to help people who are sick! What do you do?

Virginia and Lane breathe.
Virginia and Lane are in a state of silent animal warfare, a brand of warfare particular to sisters.

LANE. I'm going to splash some water on my face.
VIRGINIA. Good.

Lane exits.
From the balcony, the strains of an aria.
Ana listens to opera on the balcony, looking out over the sea.
Virginia dumps a plant on the ground and the dirt spills onto the floor.
She realizes with some surprise that she enjoys this.
Virginia makes a giant operatic mess in the living room.
Matilde enters.

MATILDE. What are you doing?
Virginia?

Virginia finishes making her operatic mess.
The aria ends.
Ana leaves the balcony.

MATILDE. *(to Virginia)* You are okay?
VIRGINIA. Actually. I feel fabulous.

Matilde sits down.

Matilde puts her head in her arms.
Lane enters.

> LANE. What the hell happened here?
> VIRGINIA. I was mad. Sorry.

Virginia flicks a piece of dirt across the room.
Lane looks at Matilde.
Matilde continues to bury her head in her arms.

> LANE. *(to Virginia)* What's wrong with her?

Virginia shrugs.

> MATILDE. It's a mess.
> VIRGINIA. I'll clean it up.
> MATILDE. Not this. Ana. Charles. It's a mess.
> LANE. Have they—fallen out of love?
> MATILDE. No.
> VIRGINIA. Is she very sick?
> MATILDE. Yes.
> LANE. Oh.
> VIRGINIA. How terrible.
> MATILDE. Yes.
> And now Charles has gone away.
> LANE. What?
> MATILDE. *(to Lane)* To Alaska.
> VIRGINIA. What?
> MATILDE. *(to Virginia)* To Alaska.
> LANE. But—why?

MATILDE. He says he's going to chop down a tree for Ana.
VIRGINIA. What?
MATILDE. A "you" tree.
He called it a you tree.

Matilde points: you.

VIRGINIA. A you tree?
MATILDE. A you tree. He says he's going to invent a new "you medicine."
VIRGINIA. My, God. He's gone crazy with love!
LANE. He's not crazy. It's a yew tree. Y-E-W. *(spelling it out.)* A Pacific Yew tree. The bark was made into Taxol. The compound prevents microtubules from decomposing. Cancer cells become so clogged with microtubules that they are slower to grow and divide.
MATILDE. He said it was a special tree.
LANE. Yes. It is a special tree.
MATILDE. He wants to plant it in the middle of Ana's courtyard. So she can smell the tree, while she's on her balcony. She won't go to the hospital. So he said he would bring the hospital to her.
VIRGINIA. That's beautiful.
LANE. It's not beautiful, Virginia. There is a woman dying, alone, while Charles chops down a fucking tree.
How heroic.
VIRGINIA. Does she need a doctor?
MATILDE. Yes. She needs a doctor.
But she won't go to the hospital. So I thought I would ask.
Do you know any doctors who go to the house?

VIRGINIA. You mean house calls?
MATILDE. Yes, house calls.

Virginia and Matilde look at Lane.

LANE. Why are you looking at me?

They continue to look at Lane.

LANE. You want me to take care of my husband's soul mate.
VIRGINIA. Look at her as a patient. Not a person.
You can do that.
LANE. If she wanted to see a doctor, she'd go to the hospital. I
am *not* going to her house. It would be totally inappropriate.

They look at Lane.
*In the distance, Charles walks slowly across the stage dressed in a parka,
looking for his tree.*
A great freezing wind.

10. Lane Makes a House Call to Her Husband's Soul Mate.

On Ana's balcony.
Lane listens to Ana's heart with a stethoscope.

LANE. Breathe in.

Breathe in again.

Lane takes off her stethoscope.

LANE. Are you having any trouble breathing?
ANA. No. But sometimes it hurts when I breathe.
LANE. Where?
ANA. Here.
LANE. Do you have pain when you're at rest?
ANA. Yes.
LANE. Where?
ANA. In my spine.
LANE. Is the pain sharp, or dull?
ANA. Sharp.
LANE. Does it radiate?
ANA. Like light?
LANE. I mean—does it move? Does it move from one place to another?
ANA. Yes. From here to there.
LANE. How's your appetite?
ANA. Not great. You must hate me.
LANE. Look—I'm being a doctor right now. That's all.

Lane palpates Ana's spine.

LANE. Does that hurt?
ANA. It hurts already.
LANE. I can't know anything without doing tests.
ANA. I know.
LANE. And you won't go to the hospital.

ANA. No.
LANE. All right.
ANA. Do you think I'm crazy?
LANE. No.
ANA. Well. Can I get you anything to drink? I have some iced tea.
LANE. Sure. Thank you.

Ana goes to get some iced tea.
Lane looks over the balcony at the sea.
She starts weeping.
Ana comes back with the iced tea.

ANA. Lane?
LANE. Oh, God! I'm *not* going to cry in front of you.
ANA. It's okay. You can cry. You must hate me.
LANE. I don't hate you.
ANA. Why are you crying?
LANE. Okay! I hate you! You—glow—with some kind of— thing—I can't *acquire* that—this thing—sort of glows off you—like a veil—in reverse—you're like *anyone's* soul mate—You have a balcony—I don't have a balcony—Charles looks at you—and he glows too—you're like two glowworms—he never looked at me like that.
ANA. Lane.
LANE. I looked at our wedding pictures to see—maybe—he looked at me that way—back then—and no—he didn't—he looked at me with *admiration*—I didn't know there was another way to be looked at—how could I know—I didn't know his face was capable of *doing that*— the way he looked at you—in my living room.

Pause.

ANA. I'm sorry.

LANE. No you're not. If you were really sorry, you wouldn't have done it.

We do as we please, and then we say we're sorry. But we're not sorry. We're just—uncomfortable—watching other people in pain.

A pause.
Ana hands Lane an iced tea.

LANE. Thank you.

They breathe.
Lane drinks her iced tea.
They both look at the fish in the bowl.

LANE. What kind of fish is that?
ANA. A fighting fish.
LANE. How old is it?
ANA. Twelve.
LANE. That's old for a fish.
ANA. I know. I keep expecting it to die. But it doesn't.

that's ... mirible [handwritten]

Lane taps on the bowl.
The fish wriggles.

ANA. How did you and Charles fall in love?
LANE. He didn't tell you?
ANA. No.

LANE. Oh. Well, we were in medical school together. We were anatomy partners. We fell in love over a dead body.

They look at each other.
Lane forgives Ana.

> ANA. Want an apple?
> LANE. Sure.

Ana gives Lane an apple.
Lane takes a bite and stops.

> LANE. Did Charles pick this apple?
> ANA. I don't know who picked it.

Lane eats the apple.

> LANE. It's good.

In the distance,
Charles walks across the stage in a heavy parka.
He carries a pick axe.
In the living room, it is snowing.

11. Lane calls Virginia.

Lane and Virginia on the telephone.

> LANE. I saw Ana.

VIRGINIA. And?

LANE. She's coming to live with me.

VIRGINIA. What?

LANE. She can't be alone. She's too sick. I invited her.

VIRGINIA. That's generous. I'm impressed.

LANE. So will you be around—during the day—to help Matilde look after her?

VIRGINIA. Oh, me? No. I got a job.

LANE. What?

VIRGINIA. I got a job.

LANE. Doing what?

VIRGINIA. I'm a checkout girl. At the grocery store.

LANE. You're not.

VIRGINIA. I am. I had my first day. I liked it. I liked using the cash register. I liked watching the vegetables go by on the conveyor belt. Purple, orange, red, green, yellow. My colleagues were nice. They didn't care if I went to Bryn Mawr. There was fellow feeling among the workers. Solidarity. And I liked it.

LANE. Wow.

VIRGINIA. So, I'm sorry. But I'll be too busy to help you.

Pause.

LANE. Wait. You made that story up.

VIRGINIA. Fine.

LANE. So you'll help me.

VIRGINIA. You want my help?

LANE. Yes.

VIRGINIA. Are you sure?

LANE. Yes.

VIRGINIA. Say: I want your help.
LANE. I want your help.
VIRGINIA. Then I'll help you.

12. Ana and Virginia. Then Matilde. Then Lane.

All of Ana's possessions have been moved into Lane's living room.
Ana's fish is in a bowl on the coffee table.
There are bags of apples on the carpet.
And luggage. With clothes spilling out of a bag.
Virginia is delivering a special tray of food for Ana.

ANA. People talk about *cancer* like it's this special thing you have a *relationship* with. And it becomes blood count, biopsy, chemotherapy, radiation, bone marrow, blah blah blah blah blah. As long as I live I want to retain my own language.

Mientras tenga vida, quiero aferrarme mi propio idioma.

No extra hospital words. I don't want a relationship with a disease. I want to have a relationship with death. That's important. But to have a relationship with a *disease*—that's some kind of bourgeois invention. And I hate it.

Virginia gives Ana the tray.

ANA. Thank you.

Ana eats a bite.

> VIRGINIA. Do you like it?
> ANA. It's delicious. What is it?
> VIRGINIA. It's a casserole. No one makes casserole anymore. I thought it might be—comforting.
> ANA. What's in it?
> VIRGINIA. Things you wouldn't want to know about.
> ANA. Well, it's good. Thank you for taking care of me, Virginia.

Virginia is moved.

> ANA. What's wrong?
> VIRGINIA. I'm not used to people thanking me.

Matilde enters, holding a telegram.
She hands it to Ana.

> MATILDE. There is a telegram. From Charles.

In the distance, Charles appears
wearing a heavy parka. Snow falls.

> CHARLES. Dear Ana. Stop. I have cut down the tree. Stop. Cannot get on plane with tree. Stop. Must learn to fly plane. Stop. Wait for me. Stop. Your beloved, Charles.

He exits.

> ANA. I want him to be a nurse and he wants to be an explorer.

Asi es la vida. *(That's life.)*

Lane enters.

>   LANE. Hi.
>   ANA. Hello!

An awkward moment.

>   VIRGINIA. Would anyone like ice cream? I made some ice
> cream.
>   LANE. You *made* it?
>   VIRGINIA. It was no trouble.
>   ANA. I love ice cream.
>   VIRGINIA. Do you like chocolate?
>   ANA. Who doesn't like chocolate. Crazy people.
>   VIRGINIA. I'll get it.
>   MATILDE. I'll help you.

Matilde and Virginia exit.
Ana and Lane sit on the couch.
Lane taps on the fishbowl.

>   LANE He made it all right.
>   ANA. He's a strong fish.

Lane taps the bowl.
The fish wriggles.
Matilde and Virginia come back with spoons.
They all eat ice cream out of the same container.

ANA. Mmmm! Amazing!
MATILDE. It must be what God eats when he is tired.
ANA. So soft.
MATILDE. Sometimes ice cream in this country is so hard.
ANA. Si.
LANE. I like ice cream.

They all eat ice cream.

ANA. Can you imagine a time before ice cream? When they couldn't keep things frozen? There was once a ship filled with ice—it sailed from Europe to South America. The ice melted by the time it got to South America. And the captain of the ship was bankrupt. All he had to sell when he got there was water.
VIRGINIA. A ship full of water.
MATILDE. A ship full of water.

Lane finishes the container of ice cream.
No one cleans up.

VIRGINIA. *(to Ana)* You look feverish. Are you warm?
ANA. I'm cold.
VIRGINIA. I'll get a thermometer.
ANA. No thermometers!
LANE. How about a blanket?
ANA. Okay. I'd like a blanket.
LANE. *(to Virginia)* Where do I keep blankets?
VIRGINIA. I'll show you.

They exit.

Matilde stays.

ANA. Matilde. My bones hurt.

MATILDE. I know they do.

ANA. Do you know what it feels like when your bones hurt?

MATILDE. No.

ANA. I hope you never know.

MATILDE. You once told me that your father killed your mother with a joke.

MATILDE. Yes.

ANA. I would like you to kill me with a joke.

MATILDE. I don't want to kill you.

I like you.

ANA. If you like me, help me.

MATILDE. What about Charles? Will you wait for him?

ANA. No.

MATILDE. Why?

ANA. I would lose all my bravery.

MATILDE. I understand.

ANA. You'll do it then?

A pause.

MATILDE. Okay.

ANA. When?

MATILDE. When you want me to.

ANA. You don't need time to make up a joke?

MATILDE. I made it up on your balcony.

ANA. Tomorrow, then.

MATILDE. Tomorrow.

Lane enters with a blanket.
She hands it to Ana.

> LANE. I hope it's warm enough.
> ANA. Thank you.
> *(to Matilde)* Good-night.
> MATILDE. *(to Ana)* Good-night.

Ana puts her head on the pillow, closing her eyes.

> MATILDE. *(whispering to Lane)* Are you coming?
> LANE. In a minute.

Matilde exits.
Lane sits on the floor and watches Ana sleep.
Lane guards Ana the way a dog would guard a rival dog,
if her rival were sick.

13. Matilde Tells Ana a Joke.

The lights turn from night to day.
Lane, Virginia, and Matilde are gathered around Ana.

ANA. I want to say good-bye to everyone before Matilde tells me a joke.
LANE. Can't I give you anything for the pain?
ANA. No. Good-bye, Lane.

LANE. Good-bye, Ana.

They embrace.

ANA. Take care of Charles.
LANE. You think I'll be taking care of him?
ANA. Of course.
LANE. Why?
ANA. You love him.
Good-bye Virginia.

Virginia weeps.

ANA. Don't cry.
Thank you for taking care of me, Virginia.

Virginia weeps.

ANA. Oh—see? That makes it worse. Oh, Virginia. I can't take it. Matilde.
Let's have the joke.
MATILDE. Are you ready?
ANA. Yes.
Everyone's always dying lying down.
I want to die standing up.

Ana stands.

ANA. The two of you had better leave the room.
I don't want you dying before your time.

They nod.
They leave.

ANA. Matilde.
Deseo el chiste ahora. *(I want the joke now.)*

The lights change.
Music.
Matilde whispers a cosmic joke in Ana's ear.
We don't hear it.
We hear sublime music instead.
A subtitle projects:

The funniest joke in the world.

Ana laughs and laughs.
Ana collapses.
Matilde kneels beside her.
Matilde wails.

MATILDE. Ohh—

Lane and Virginia rush in.
Lane checks Ana's pulse.
The women look at one another.

VIRGINIA. What do we do?
LANE. I don't know.
VIRGINIA. You're the doctor!
LANE. I've never seen someone die in a house before.

Only in a hospital.
Where they clean everything up.
VIRGINIA. What do the nurses do?
MATILDE. They close the eyes.
LANE. That's right.

Matilde closes Ana's eyes.

MATILDE. And they wash the body.
LANE. I'll wash her.

Lane goes to get a towel
and a bowl of water.

VIRGINIA. Should we say a prayer?
MATILDE. You say a prayer, Virginia.
A prayer cleans the air the way water cleans the dirt.
VIRGINIA. Ana. I hope you are apple picking.

Lane enters with a bowl of water.
She washes Ana's body.
Time slows down.

Suddenly, from off-stage:

CHARLES. Ana!

Charles pounds on the door.

CHARLES. Ana! Ana!

The women look at one another.
Charles walks in carrying an enormous tree.
The tree reaches all the way up to the balcony.
Charles is sweating and breathing as though
he has carried his tree great distances.
Lane goes to Charles.

> CHARLES. I brought back this tree.
> I went to the other house—but no one was—
> It won't help?
> LANE. No.
> CHARLES. Why?
> LANE. Charles.
> CHARLES. You were here?
> LANE. Yes.
> CHARLES. Can I see her?

Lane nods.

> LANE. Charles?

Lane kisses Charles on the forehead.

> CHARLES. Thank you. Will you hold my tree?
> LANE. Yes.

Lane holds the tree.
The light changes.
Charles moves towards Ana's body
as the lights come up on Matilde.

14. Matilde.

Matilde, to the audience.

> MATILDE. This is how I imagine my parents.
> My mother is about to give birth to me.
> The hospital is too far away.
> My mother runs up a hill in December and says: now!
> My mother is lying down under a tree.
> My father is telling her a joke to try and keep her calm.

Ana and Charles become Matilde's mother and father.
Matilde's father whispers a joke in Portuguese to her mother.

> MATILDE. My mother laughed. She laughed so hard that
> I popped out.
> My mother said I was the only baby who laughed when
> I came into the world.
> She said I was laughing at my father's joke.
> I laughed to take in the air.
> I took in some air, and then I cried.

A moment of completion between Matilde and her parents.

> I think maybe heaven is a sea of untranslatable jokes.
> Only everyone is laughing.

The End

PRODUCTION NOTES

DOUBLE CASTING

It is important that Ana and Charles play Matilde's mother and father
in the first act. How much can they create, without speaking, a sense
of memory and longing, through silence and gesture? Ana's transfor-
mation at the end of the play should create a full circle for Matilde,
from the dead to the living and back again.

SUBTITLES

The director might consider projecting subtitles in the play for some
scene titles and some stage directions. I would suggest these:

A woman tells a joke in Portuguese (page 7)

Lane. (page 7)

Virginia. (page 8)

Matilde. (page 9)

*Virginia and Lane experience a primal moment in which they
are 7 and 9 years old.* (page 25)
Matilde tries to think up the perfect joke. (page 26)
Matilde tries to think up the perfect joke. (page 28)

Virginia has a deep impulse to order the universe. (page 30)
Charles performs surgery on the woman he loves. (page 41)
Ana. (page 42)

Charles. (page 43)
They fall in love. (page 45)
They fall in love some more. (page 45)
They fall in love completely. (page 45)
Ana's balcony. (page 55)
Matilde tries to think up the perfect joke. (page 58)
Lane makes a house-call to her husband's soul mate. (page 70)
Lane forgives Ana. (page 74)
Lane calls Virginia. (page 74)
Lane guards Ana the way a dog would guard a rival dog, if her rival were sick. (page 81)
The funniest joke in the world. (page 83)

PRONUNCIATION

Matilde is pronounced by the Americans in the play as Matilda. It is pronounced by Ana as Mathilda until she realizes that Matilde is Brazilian. And it is pronounced by Matilde and the more observant characters in the play as Ma-chil-gee, the correct Brazilian pronunciation.

JOKES

I want the choice of jokes to be open, allowing for the possibility that different productions may come up with different and more perfect Brazilian jokes. So please use these jokes as you will.

Joke #1, to be told on page 7

Um homem tava a ponto de casar e ele tava muito nervosa ao preparar-se pra noite de nupias porque ele nunca tuvo sexo en la vida de ele. Enton ele vai pra médico e pergunta: "O que que eu devo fazor?" O médico fala: "Não se preocupa. Voce coloca uma nota de dez dolares na bolso direito y voce practica 10, 10, 10."

Enton el homen vai pra casa y practica todo semana 10,10,10. Aí ele volta pra médico y lhe fala: "Muito bem! Agora você coloca uma nota de 10 no bolso direito e uma nota do 20 (vinte) no bolso esquerdo e practica: "10, 20; 10, 20."

Ele foi pra casa praticou toda semana 10,20; 10,20; 10,20. Ele volta pra medico y ele falou: "É isso aí! Agora você coloca uma nota de 10 no bolso direito, uma de 20 no bolso esquerdo e uma de 100 (cem) na frente. Aí você practica: 10, 20, 100.

Aí ele casou. A noite de núpcias chegou. Ele tava con sua mulher todo bonita e gustosa e ele comencou a fazer amor "10, 20, 100; 10, 20, 100; 10—20—Ai, que se foda o trocado: 100, 100, 100!!!"

Translation:

A man is getting married. He's never had sex and he's very nervous about his wedding night. So, he goes to a doctor and he says, "I'm really nervous, what should I do?" The doctor says, "Don't worry about it. Go home and put a ten dollar bill in your right pocket and you practice 10! 10! 10!, moving your hips to the left." So, he goes home and after a week of practice, he returns to the doctor who says "Very good. Now, go back home and put a ten dollar bill in your right hand pocket, a twenty dollar bill in your left hand pocket and go 10! 20! 10! 20!" *(The joke teller moves hips from side to side)* So, he practices, does very well, returns to the doctor who says "Perfect! Now you're going to put a 10 dollar bill in your left hand pocket, a 20 dollar bill in your right hand pocket and a 100 dollar bill in front, where you will go like this 10! 20! 100!!" The man practices as he is told, goes back to the doctor who says "Perfect! You're ready to go!" The big day arrives and the man is very excited about his night with his wife. The time comes and he is in bed and he starts with his wife 10! 20! 100! 10! 20! 100! 10! 20—Oh, fuck the change 100! 100! 100!

Joke #2, to be told on page 38

Por que os homens na cama são como comida de microondas? Estão prontos em trinta segundos.

Translation:

Why are men in bed like microwave food? They're done in thirty seconds.

Joke #3, to be told on page 50

O melhor investimento que existe é comprar um argentino pelo valor que ele vale e depois vendê-lo pelo valor que ele acha que vale.

Translation:

The best investment ever is to buy an Argentinean for what he is really worth and later sell him for what he thinks he is worth.

ABOUT THE AUTHOR

Sarah Ruhl's plays include *The Clean House* (Pulitzer Prize Finalist, 2005; The Susan Smith Blackburn Prize, 2004); *Passion Play: A Cycle* (The Fourth Freedom Forum Playwriting Award from The Kennedy Center and a Helen Hayes Awards nomination for best new play), *Dead Man's Cell Phone, Melancholy Play, Eurydice, Orlando* and *Late: A Cowboy Song.* Her plays have been produced at Lincoln Center Theater, Goodman Theatre, Arena Stage, Woolly Mammoth Theatre Company, South Coast Repertory Theater, Yale Rep., Berkeley Rep., The Wilma Theater, Actors Theatre of Louisville, Madison Rep. and the Piven Theatre, among others. Her plays have also been produced in London, Germany, Australia, Canada and Israel, and have been translated into Polish, Russian, Spanish, Norwegian, Korean and German.

Originally from Chicago, Ms. Ruhl received her M.F.A. from Brown University, where she studied with Paula Vogel. In 2003, she was the recipient of the Helen Merrill Emerging Playwrights Award and the Whiting Writers' Award. She is a member of 13P and New Dramatists and recently won the MacArthur Fellowship.